Cãtastrophe

'Caterpillar Catastrophe'
An original concept by Jenny Moore
© Jenny Moore

Illustrated by Esther Hernando

Published by MAVERICK ARTS PUBLISHING LTD

Studio 11, City Business Centre, 6 Brighton Road,

Horsham, West Sussex, RH13 5BB

© Maverick Arts Publishing Limited November 2020

+44 (0)1403 256941

A CIP catalogue record for this book is available at the British Library.

ISBN 978-1-84886-728-4

www.maverickbooks.co.uk

This book is rated as: Lime Band (Guided Reading)

Caterpillar Catastrophe

Written by **Jenny Moore**   Illustrated by
Esther Hernando

Chapter 1

Leroy was walking down the alley to Grandad's back garden when he heard a horrible wailing noise.

"Oo-ah-oo-oo-oo."

It sounded like a chimpanzee with tummy ache... and it was growing louder with every step. Leroy followed the sound all the way to Grandad's garden and peered over the wall.

It wasn't a chimpanzee with tummy troubles. It was Grandad, singing to his vegetables.

"Oo-ah-oo-oo-oo," Grandad wailed at the top of his voice. "It's growing time for you-oo-oo.

Listen to my cabbage song,

Grow fat and round,

Grow big and strong..."

"Hello," called Leroy, with his hands over his ears.

"Oh, hello," said Grandad, opening the gate for him. "I was just singing my cabbages a little song to help them grow faster. You can help if you want."

"Erm... Have you got any other jobs we could do together?" Leroy asked. Grandad's singing was more likely to *kill* the cabbages.

"You bet," said Grandad. "I've got a list of jobs as long as my arm. It's the Glenford Gardening Competition on Saturday," he explained. "The winner gets to be on the local news! How amazing would that be? Plus I really want to beat grumpy Mr Tomkins from next door." He added in a whisper, "I've even ordered a secret weapon on the internet. If you take over the singing for me, I'll go and fetch it."

Grandad hurried off to his shed, leaving Leroy to entertain the vegetables.

"Yo, listen up all,

To my new cabbage rap,

This is DJ Leroy

In the vegetable patch.

If you want to be big

And star on local TV,

You'd better flex those leaves

And get growing with me..."

Grandad came back from the shed, clutching a small green bottle. He shook his hips and waggled his bottom in time to Leroy's beat.

"Oo-ah-oo-oo-oo," he joined in. "It's growing time for..."

"That's enough!" came an angry roar, making them both jump.

Chapter 2

Grandad's grumpy neighbour, Mr Tomkins, glared at them over the fence. His cheeks were red with anger.

"Stop that terrible racket," he growled. "Or I'll report you to the police for crimes against my ears."

"Sorry," said Leroy. "We were just getting ready for the gardening competition."

"Well you're wasting your time," said Mr Tomkins. "If anyone's going to win that competition, it's me." He stomped off, out of sight.

"Huh! We'll show him," whispered Grandad, handing Leroy the small green bottle he'd fetched from the shed. "I think it's time for my secret weapon."

Leroy examined the label. "*Grow Magic*," he read. "*For bigger, better plants and flowers. Add one drop to your watering can for magical results.* Wow! Will it work?"

"There's only one way to find out," said Grandad. "Let's get watering."

Tring-tring, came the sound of the phone. *Tring-tring*.

"Oh bother," said Grandad. "That might be one of my yoga students. I'd better go and answer it."

"Don't worry," said Leroy. "I'll add the Grow Magic and do the watering while you talk to them."

Grandad gave him a thumbs-up. "Brilliant. Just one drop, remember," he called as he hurried towards the house. "It's powerful stuff."

Leroy filled the watering can, imagining how furious Mr Tomkins would be when they won. He added some Grow Magic, daydreaming about

starring on the local news with Grandad. They'd

be famous! But he was so busy daydreaming he

tipped in the whole bottle by mistake!

Uh-oh. Leroy didn't know what to do. There

was no sign of Grandad, so he emptied the

watering can over the cabbages and beans and

hoped for the best.

Chapter 3

Leroy was worried. What if Grandad's plants withered and died? What if he'd killed them with too much Grow Magic? He held his breath and waited, but nothing happened. *Phew!* He filled

another watering can for the roses. There was no more Grow Magic left to feed them, so he treated them to another verse of his rap instead.

"Hey there roses,

All pretty and red,

Smelling so nice

In your flowerbed,

Stretch your petals

And reach for the skies—

We need to help Grandad

Win first prize…"

Leroy jumped as someone tapped him on the shoulder. He span round, but there was nobody there… just an enormous bean, bobbing in the breeze.

"Wowzers!" cried Leroy, gazing up at the giant swaying beanstalk. It was like something out of a fairy tale! "Double wowzers," he cried as he spotted Grandad's cabbages. They were already the size of beach balls and were still growing. That bottle of Grow Magic really *must* have been magic after all.

He ran to fetch Grandad. "You'll never believe what's happened," he panted.

Leroy was right. Grandad *couldn't* believe it. He rubbed his eyes in amazement. "I must be dreaming," he said.

"It's no dream, Grandad," Leroy told him. "I can see them too. And when the judges see them, we're *bound* to win the competition. We'll be famous!"

Grandad grinned. "I *told* you singing was good for plants!" And with that he was off again, dancing round the lawn in excitement.

"Oo-ah-oo-oo-ah," he warbled,

"I'm going to be a garden star,

On the news with my grandson,

It's going to be such fun, fun, fun!"

There was a loud snort of anger from the other side of the fence. "How many times do I have to ask you to be quiet?" growled Mr Tomkins. "I've a good mind to..." When he saw Grandad's enormous vegetables, his mouth hung open like a surprised goldfish.

Chapter 4

Leroy danced along after Grandad with his hands

over his ears.

"I don't think it was your singing that made them grow," he shouted. "It was the—" Leroy stopped. *Wait a minute*, he thought.

Crunch.

What was *that?*

Crunch, crunch, crunch.

"Uh-oh," Leroy said, pointing at the cabbages.

"I must have watered some caterpillars too. Look at them, they're enormous!"

Leroy and Grandad stared in horror at the giant wriggling beasts chomping their way through the vegetable patch.

"My poor cabbages!" wailed Grandad.

"Don't worry," Leroy said. "I'll help you get rid of them." He paused. "How *do* you get rid of caterpillars?"

"I usually pick them off with my fingers," said Grandad. "Then I pop them over the fence as a present for Mr Tomkins," he added with a cheeky wink. "But we can't do that with these brutes. The hairs on their backs are too prickly."

Leroy thought for a moment. "I know just the thing. Follow me!" he cried, running into the house.

Leroy made suits of armour out of cooking

pans and baking trays, with cling film and foil to hold everything in place. He and Grandad looked like crazy kitchen knights!

"Don't forget your hand protectors, Sir Grandad," Leroy joked, passing over a pair of bright yellow oven gloves.

"Thank you, Sir Leroy," said Grandad, waving a wooden spoon in the air like a sword. "Let's go!"

They raced back to the cabbage patch. The caterpillars had grown even bigger. Leroy and Grandad pulled and heaved. They huffed and puffed, tugging with all their might. It was no good though. The caterpillars were too big and

strong... and they were *still* growing.

Chapter 5

"I'll never be on the news now," sighed Grandad, shaking his head sadly. "There'll be no garden left!"

The caterpillars were bigger than ever, but Leroy refused to give up. There must be *some* way of stopping them.

"The hose!" he cried. "That's it! If we can't *pull* the caterpillars off, we'll *blast* them off instead."

Grandad high-fived him. "Great idea! You grab the nozzle and get ready to spray. I'll turn the tap on as hard as it will go."

Leroy took up position, aiming the hose at Caterpillar Number One.

Pshhhhhhhh! Water came squirting out at full blast. But the caterpillar was too clever.

With one flick of its back legs, it knocked the hose right out of Leroy's hands.

Pssshhhhh! The hose shot off round the garden, spraying water everywhere.

Mr Tomkins peered over the fence. "*Now what's going on?*" he demanded.

Pssshhhhhh! The runaway jet of water hit him

in the face, leaving him dripping with rage.

"How dare you?" he roared. "I'm soaking."

Leroy tried not to laugh. "I'm really sorry," he said, as Grandad switched off the tap. "We were trying to get rid of the giant caterpillars. I watered them with a bottle of Grow Magic and now they won't *stop* growing."

"Grow Magic?" snarled Mr Tomkins, waving his fist at Grandad. "I've a good mind to report you to the competition judges for cheating. Let's see how well you do *then*." Mr Tomkins stomped off again.

"Oh no," said Leroy. "What if you get thrown out of the competition?" He ducked, as an enormous caterpillar swayed towards him with a hungry gleam in its eyes.

"I'm more worried about getting *eaten*," replied Grandad. "What if they get bored of chewing plants and start chewing *us?*"

Chapter 6

"It's time to call in the experts," said Grandad. "Hide in the greenhouse while I get my mobile and some biscuits. We should be safe in there."

It was hot inside the greenhouse. Leroy peeped out from behind the tomato plants while Grandad sprinted back to the house for his phone. The caterpillars were growing *again*. There was no stopping them!

"Hello," said Grandad, talking into his phone as he joined Leroy in the greenhouse. "Is that The Big Bug Squad? We've got a bit of a caterpillar emergency here. A *giant* caterpillar emergency, I mean... Yes, that's right. Come as quickly as you can."

Leroy and Grandad shared a packet of chocolate biscuits while they waited for help to arrive.

"Look," said Leroy, pointing past the tomatoes towards the nearest caterpillar. "Something's happening. I think it's turning into a cocoon."

"You're right," agreed Grandad. "It looks like they've reached the chrysalis stage already. The Grow Magic must have sped everything up. Hopefully that means they've stopped eating my garden!"

By the time The Big Bug Squad arrived with their bug zappers, there were no caterpillars left to zap. There was just a row of hard green cases hanging off the giant beanstalk.

"I'm sorry," Grandad told the Big Bug boss. "I don't think we're going to need you after all. Look! They're not caterpillars anymore."

"We could zap them anyway," offered the boss as he helped himself to a biscuit.

Leroy shook his head. "No. We don't want to hurt them if we don't have to. Besides, I've got a much better idea..."

Chapter 7

It was Saturday. Leroy and Grandad were just putting the final touches to the garden when Mr Tomkins peered over the fence.

"There's no point doing that now," he gloated, holding up his winner's rosette. "The competition's over. It's such a shame you got caught cheating."

Grandad and Leroy took no notice. They just smiled.

"The local news team will be coming to film me in my winning garden any minute now," boasted Mr Tomkins. "In fact, this looks like them now!" He pointed to the long line of reporters streaming along the alley towards his garden with their cameras and fluffy microphones.

Grandad and Leroy smiled even harder. "That looks like a *national* news team to me," said Grandad.

Mr Tomkins puffed out his chest. "*National* television? You'd better not spoil the interview with your awful singing. This way!" he shouted to the news crew. "Welcome to my winning garden!"

But the news crew walked straight on past his gate... it was Grandad they'd come to see.

"Welcome to my garden," said Grandad. "This is my grandson, Leroy, and these are the famous giant butterflies."

"We're expecting them to hatch any moment now," added Leroy.

"How about some tea and biscuits while we wait?" Grandad offered. "Or we could show you our new caterpillar song? I'm sure everyone at home would love to hear that!"

Mr Tomkins spluttered with rage as Leroy and Grandad danced round the garden, rapping for

the cameras.

"Now listen up viewers

And listen up well,

It's Leroy and Grandad

With a story to tell,

About the biggest ever bugs

In the vegetable patch...

Woah, look everybody—

They're starting to hatch!"

Discussion Points

1. Why did the caterpillars become giant in the story?

2. Who did Leroy splash water over when he was trying to blast the caterpillars off the plants?

a) Himself

b) Grandad

c) Mr Tomkins

3. What was your favourite part of the story?

4. What was Grandad doing when Leroy arrived in the garden at the beginning of the story?

5. Why do you think Leroy stopped the Big Bug Squad at the end of the story?

6. Who was your favourite character and why?

7. There were moments in the story when Leroy made **mistakes**. How does he deal with this?

8. What do you think happens after the end of the story?

Book Bands for Guided Reading

The Institute of Education book banding system is a scale of colours that reflects the various levels of reading difficulty. The bands are assigned by taking into account the content, the language style, the layout and phonics. Word, phrase and sentence level work is also taken into consideration.

The Maverick Readers Scheme is a bright, attractive range of books covering the pink to grey bands. All of these books have been book banded for guided reading to the industry standard and edited by a leading educational consultant.

To view the whole Maverick Readers scheme, visit our website at
www.maverickearlyreaders.com

Or scan the QR code to view our scheme instantly!

Pink
Red
Yellow
Blue
Green
Orange
Turquoise
Purple
Gold
White
Lime
Brown
Grey

Maverick Chapter Readers
(From Lime to Grey Band)